For Mom, Dad, Maryellen, Brian, John, Bobby and Joey.

Stephen Parlato

The WORLD that LOVED BOOKS

SIMPLY READ BOOKS

here once was a world where everyone loved books, even the animals.

Everyone loved to read so much that when they read their books, they became what they read.

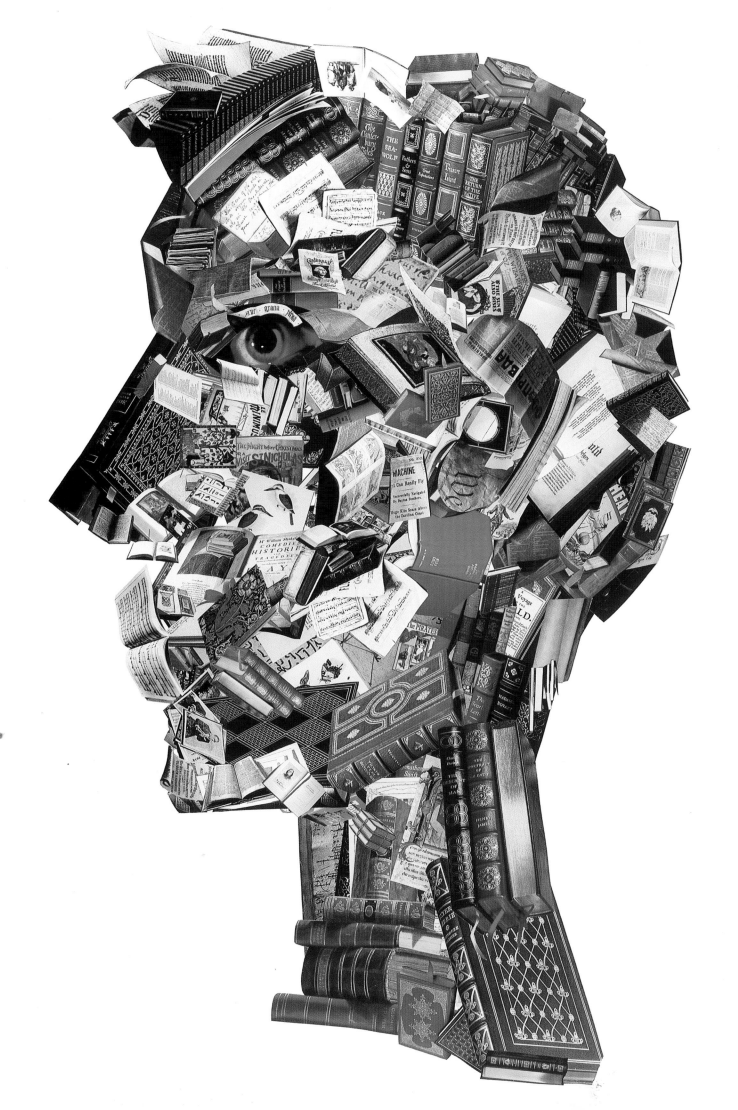

A man reading about flowers... became flowers.

A man reading about insects and bugs became *Insects and bugs.*

A rabbit reading about turtles
became *turtles,*

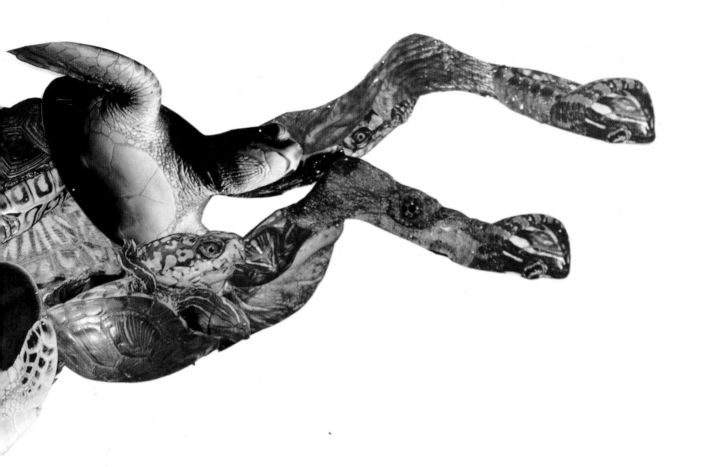

his perfect little cottontail

now a sea turtle's flipper.

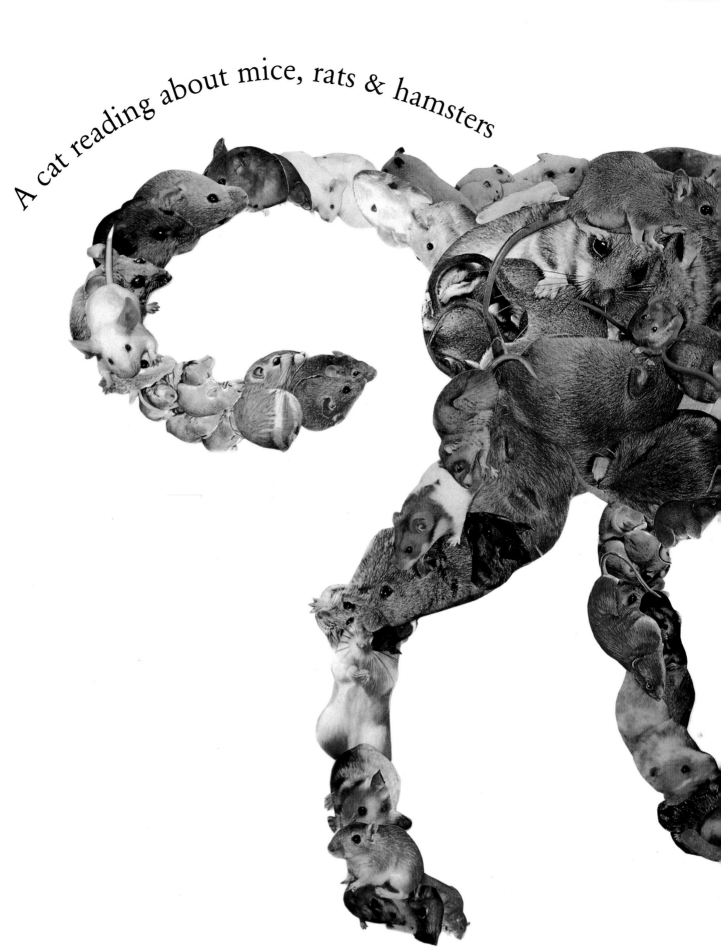

A cat reading about mice, rats & hamsters

soon had many *tales* to tell.

A woman reading about angels

became *choirs of angels.*

A dragon reading about treasure
became a treasure trove of gold
and diamonds and pearls.

He felt all polished and *shiny* and new.

A man reading about snakes and lizards found it s-s-s-s-s-s-s-s-so s-s-s-s-s-s-s-scientific he thought it was s-s-s-s-s-s-s-s-s-s-s simply terrific.

When the man's friend, a horse, borrowed his book about snakes and lizards,

it simply gave him the *shivers.*

A dinosaur reading about frogs
and salamanders became

frogs & salamanders.

He found the book to be very

ribbiting.

A woman reading about birds in a lightning storm

became *birds* fleeing a **storm**.

A rhinoceros reading about
butterflies and caterpillars
grew so many *beautiful wings*

that it made his friend the little bird *quite jealous.*

The horse read a book
about fish and thought
it was *fintastic*.

She bought a copy as a present for her friend

who also found it a *Swimmingly* good read.

The man who received the book on fish bought a book of rabbit, chipmunk, and squirrel tales and sent it to his friend the horse as his way of saying, *"thanks."*

The horse then wanted to read more,
so she went to the public library
and borrowed a book
about flags.

She was feeling so *proud,*
waving even at strangers.

She enjoyed it so much
she was one day late
returning the book and
had to pay a fine.

The End

First published in 2008 by Simply Read Books
www.simplyreadbooks.com

Text & illustrations © 2008 Stephen Parlato

CATALOGUING IN PUBLICATION DATA

Parlato, Stephen, 1954-
The world that loved books / Stephen Parlato.

ISBN 978-1-894965-98-9

    I. Title.

PZ7.P23Wo 2008   j813'.6   C2008-900768-9

Book design by Elisa Gutiérrez

10 9 8 7 6 5 4 3 2 1

Printed in Singapore